nickelodeon™

NICKELODEON NURSERY RHYMES

 A GOLDEN BOOK • NEW YORK

www.randomhouse.com/kids
Educators and librarians, for a variety of teaching tools, visit us at www.randomhouse.com/teachers
ISBN: 978-0-375-87377-5
Printed in the United States of America
10 9 8 7 6 5 4 3 2 1

Little Miss Dora,
A brave, bold explorer,
Explored the rainforest one day.
Along came a spider,
Who sat down beside her,
And Dora said, "¡Hola! Let's play!"

Patty cook, patty cook, move that pan.
Flip me a patty as high as you can.
Toss it and catch it.
Now I've got a feeling—
That patty, I think,
Is stuck to the ceiling.

Hickory, dickory, dock!
Hoho jumped over the clock.
The clock struck ten,
He jumped again.
Hickory, dickory, dock!

The Wonder Pets all saved a farm. E-I-E-I-O!
And on this farm there was a pig. E-I-E-I-O!
With an *oink, oink* here
And an *oink, oink* there.
Here an *oink,* there an *oink,*
Everywhere an *oink, oink.*
The Wonder Pets all saved a farm. E-I-E-I-O!

The Wonder Pets all saved a farm. E-I-E-I-O!
And on this farm there was a cow. E-I-E-I-O!
With a *moo, moo* here
And a *moo, moo* there.
Here a *moo,* there a *moo,*
Everywhere a *moo, moo.*
The Wonder Pets all saved a farm. E-I-E-I-O!

The Wonder Pets all saved a farm. E-I-E-I-O!
And on this farm there was a duck. E-I-E-I-O!
With a *quack, quack* here
And a *quack, quack* there.
Here a *quack*, there a *quack*,
Everywhere a *quack, quack*.
The Wonder Pets all saved a farm. E-I-E-I-O!

The Wonder Pets all saved a farm. E-I-E-I-O!
And how it worked was with teamwork. E-I-E-I-O!
With some teamwork here
And some teamwork there.
Here teamwork, there teamwork,
Everywhere teamwork works.
The Wonder Pets all saved a farm. E-I-E-I-O!

Sail, sail, sail our ship
Gently on the sea.
Merrily, merrily,
Merrily, merrily—
Where could treasure be?

Hike, hike,
Hike along—
My, this island's hot!
Searching, searching,
Searching, searching—
X will mark the spot!

Dig, dig, dig right here.
Taking turns is best.
Merrily, merrily,
Merrily, merrily—
We found a treasure chest!

It's raining, it's pouring.
Rintoo says it's boring.
But Kai-lan says, "Let's go outside
And splash in the puddles all morning!"

Little BobPeep has lost his sheep,
So around the town he wheels.
He looks high and low, but a strong undertow
Pulls him to Jellyfish Fields.

There was an animal rescuer,
And Diego was his name-o.
D-I-E-G-O! D-I-E-G-O!
D-I-E-G-O!
And Diego was his name-o.

There was a boy who hopped on logs,
And Diego was his name-o.
[CLAP]-I-E-G-O!
[CLAP]-I-E-G-O!
[CLAP]-I-E-G-O!
And Diego was his name-o.

There was a boy who saved a sloth,
And Diego was his name-o.
[CLAP]-[CLAP]-E-G-O!
[CLAP]-[CLAP]-E-G-O!
[CLAP]-[CLAP]-E-G-O!
And Diego was his name-o.

There was a boy who found wolf pups,
And Diego was his name-o.
[CLAP]-[CLAP]-[CLAP]-G-O!
[CLAP]-[CLAP]-[CLAP]-G-O!
[CLAP]-[CLAP]-[CLAP]-G-O!
And Diego was his name-o.

There was a boy who helped his friends,
And Diego was his name-o.
[CLAP]-[CLAP]-[CLAP]-[CLAP]-O!
[CLAP]-[CLAP]-[CLAP]-[CLAP]-O!
[CLAP]-[CLAP]-[CLAP]-[CLAP]-O!
And Diego was his name-o.

Here we go round the banana tree,
The banana tree, the banana tree.
Here we go round the banana tree
So early in the morning.

Head, shoulders, knees and toes, knees and toes.

Head, shoulders, knees and toes, knees and toes.

Eyes

and ears

and mouth

and nose.

Head, shoulders, knees and toes, knees and toes.

Pandy bear, pandy bear, turn around.
Pandy bear, pandy bear, touch the ground.
Pandy bear, pandy bear, I love you.
Pandy bear, pandy bear loves me, too!

Boots, be nimble.
Boots, fly high.
Boots, swing on
The leafy vine!

Rub-a-dub-dub, three pets in a tub,
Who do you think they could be?
A duckling, a turtle, a guinea pig, too—
And all of them have celery!

I know a troll who's a grumpy old soul,
The Grumpy Old Troll is he.
He lives by a bridge and asks for a toll
With riddles that are really tricky.

YeYe, YeYe, please won't you say
How does your garden grow?
"I plant the seeds and pull the weeds,
And water and rake and hoe."

Hey, diddle, diddle,
Isa plays the fiddle,
And Benny is strumming a tune.
Dora did say, "This fiesta's the best!
But Swiper ran away with my spoon!"

My Krabby Patty was juicy and tall.
My Krabby Patty had a great fall.
SpongeBob the fry cook and all of his friends
Couldn't put my poor Patty together again!

The itsy bitsy spider
Got stuck in a waterspout.
The Wonder Pets flew in
to help the spider out.
With a little teamwork,
The spider tried again.
And the Wonder Pets shared celery
With their spider friend.

If you're super happy and you know it, clap your hands.
If you're super happy and you know it, clap your hands.
If you're super happy and you know it,
And you really want to show it,
If you're super happy and you know it, clap your hands!

SpongeBob had a jellyfish.
Its sting could make you crow.
Everywhere that SpongeBob went
That jellyfish would go.
It followed him to school one day,
Which was against the rules.
It made the students duck and hide,
That jellyfish at school.

Silly, silly Patrick Star,
SpongeBob wonders where you are.
Down below the sea so deep,
Underneath your rock you sleep.
Cozy, cozy Patrick Star,
SpongeBob now knows where you are.